Dear Parent:

Congratulations! Your child is taking the first steps on an exciting journey. The destination? Independent reading!

STEP INTO READING® will help your child get there. The program offers five steps to reading success. Each step includes fun stories and colorful art. There are also Step into Reading Sticker Books, Step into Reading Math Readers, Step into Reading Write-In Readers, Step into Reading Phonics Readers, and Step into Reading Phonics First Steps! Boxed Sets—a complete literacy program with something for every child.

Learning to Read, Step by Step!

Ready to Read Preschool–Kindergarten
• big type and easy words • rhyme and rhythm • picture clues
For children who know the alphabet and are eager to begin reading.

Reading with Help Preschool–Grade 1
• basic vocabulary • short sentences • simple stories
For children who recognize familiar words and sound out new words with help.

Reading on Your Own Grades 1–3
• engaging characters • easy-to-follow plots • popular topics
For children who are ready to read on their own.

Reading Paragraphs Grades 2–3
• challenging vocabulary • short paragraphs • exciting stories
For newly independent readers who read simple sentences with confidence.

Ready for Chapters Grades 2–4
• chapters • longer paragraphs • full-color art
For children who want to take the plunge into chapter books but still like colorful pictures.

STEP INTO READING® is designed to give every child a successful reading experience. The grade levels are only guides. Children can progress through the steps at their own speed, developing confidence in their reading, no matter what their grade.

Remember, a lifetime love of reading starts with a single step!

Thomas the Tank Engine & Friends
A Britt Allcroft Company Production THE BRITT ALLCROFT COMPANY

Based on The Railway Series by The Rev. W. Awdry.
Copyright © 1990 Gullane (Thomas) LLC. All rights reserved under International and
Pan-American Copyright Conventions. Published in the United States by Random House
Children's Books, a division of Random House, Inc., New York, and simultaneously in Canada
by Random House of Canada Limited, Toronto.

www.stepintoreading.com

www.thomasthetankengine.com

Educators and librarians, for a variety of teaching tools, visit us at
www.randomhouse.com/teachers

Library of Congress Cataloging-in-Publication Data
Awdry, W. Happy birthday, Thomas! / illustrated by Owain Bell.
    p. cm. — (Step into reading. A step 2 book)
Based on the Railway series by the Rev. W. Awdry.
SUMMARY: Thomas the train engine thinks that all the other engines are too busy to help him
celebrate his birthday, but he is in for a surprise.
ISBN 0-679-80809-4 (trade) — ISBN 0-679-90809-9 (lib. bdg.)
[1. Birthdays—Fiction. 2. Parties—Fiction. 3. Railroads—Trains—Fiction.]
I. Bell, Owain, ill. II. Awdry, W. Railway series. III. Title.
IV. Series: Step into reading. Step 2 book.
PZ7.A9613 Hap 2003 [E]—dc21 2002013766

Printed in the United States of America 47 46 45

STEP INTO READING, RANDOM HOUSE, and the Random House colophon are registered trademarks
of Random House, Inc.

Happy Birthday, THOMAS!

Based on The Railway Series
by the Rev. W. Awdry
illustrated by Owain Bell

Random House 🏠 New York

"Peep! Peep!"
Here comes
Thomas the Tank Engine.

Thomas and his friends work hard every day.

Thomas does not want
to work today.

It is his birthday!

He wants a party,

with presents,

balloons,

and silly hats.

MEN AT WORK

But Sir Topham Hatt says,
"Henry is busy.
Gordon is busy.
James is busy.

You <u>must</u> work today,
Thomas."

So off Thomas goes
to his branch line.

Back and forth.

Back and forth.

He carries people.

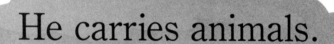

He carries animals.

He carries wood.

He carries grain.

Thomas sees his friends
near the engine shed.
No one says,
"Happy birthday."

No one says a word
about presents,
balloons,
or silly hats.

At the end
of the day
Thomas heads home.

"Those engines did not look so busy to <u>me</u>."

Oh no!

A cow is in the way.

"Move!" says Thomas.

"Moo," says the cow.

"No, no, no!"
says Thomas.
"Not <u>moo</u>. MOVE!"

At last the cow moves.

Thomas is late.

Thomas is tired.

Some birthday!

Sir Topham Hatt opens the doors to the dark shed.

Thomas chugs inside.

Lights come on.

"Surprise!"

say all Thomas's friends.

"We <u>were</u> busy,"

says Henry.

"We were busy making
a party for you!"
says James.

It is a wonderful party.

There are presents,

balloons,

and silly hats to wear.

Happy birthday, Thomas!